Berwick Crimes & Punishment
in the 17th-19th Centuries

by

Berwick U3A Creative Writers

This is a book of short stories; works of fiction, each set by its author in an historical context around actual recorded events.

Cover Photo: © Berwick Archives

Printed and bound by Martins the Printers, Berwick-upon-Tweed
www.martins-the-printers.com

This book is dedicated to the memory of

Mavis Maureen Raper MBE (1930 – 2019).

Maureen encouraged and supported many members of Berwick U3A Creative Writers over the years in their quest to develop writing skills.

Just before Maureen passed away, she had planned with Linda Bankier to introduce us to the Berwick Archives, enabling us to complete the project so dear to her heart and which is the subject of this book.

This is our tribute to her.

Maureen was our inspirational mentor and guide. We hope we have done her proud.

Acknowledgements

This book would not have been possible without the time, patience and help given by the following people: -

Linda Bankier, the Berwick Archivist, was invaluable in showing us how to conduct our research in the Archives. Linda gave us guidance, her expertise and more than a few pointers to tease out cases in the Berwick Petty and Quarter Sessions of the 17th – 19th centuries.

Eddie Matthews for providing information and support

Chris O'Neil and **Angela Darling** for editing and proofreading our draft stories.

Homer Lindsay for book edit, assembly and pre-print preparation of the manuscript.

Graham Campbell of Martins the Printers for helping to bring our project to fruition.

Grateful thanks to you all.

Contributors

The authors of the stories in this book are all members of Berwick U3A Creative Writing Group.

Veronica Burningham

E. P. Mack

Alan Dumble

Homer Lindsay

Stella McLaren

Angela Winson

Contents

John Smithson Vicar of Berwick 1672
My last sermon
by Stella McLaren

Wednesday August 24th 1672 dawned to the sound of a horse whinnying, voices, the words muffled. Then heavy footsteps sounded on the roughhewn flag stones, filling him with dread. The time had come.

In 1648 Oliver Cromwell allowed Berwick to build a Parish church. Nothing ornate, no spires or bell towers, just something simple. It was completed in 1652 but not consecrated until July 1662. Berwick in the 17th century was administered by the Freemen having been granted a Royal Charter in April 1604 by James the V1 of Scotland and the 1st of England. Berwick itself wasn't a particularly lawless town, mostly petty crime and drunken revelry at the weekends. Once in a while though the unthinkable happened. A murder. All the more shocking when it was committed by the last person you would expect. It is here our story begins.

In July 1661 a young man John Smithson, being of average height and build, fairly non-descript really, was appointed as assistant minister to the newly finished Holy Trinity church. He had served for 3 years, until being appointed as minister in 1664. It was during that time he met his soon to be wife Sarah (Rosden) Moore.

Saturday 11th October dawned dry and bright. Sarah being excited and no doubt apprehensive, for today was her wedding day. Her carefree life as she knew it was to be changed forever. She was marrying John the vicar of Holy Trinity, in that very church. Sarah was to be embarking on a whole new kind of responsibility as the vicar's wife. For the next few months they were a happy couple and their joy was made complete when, on the 18th August 1665, Sarah gave birth to a son who they named Charles. The couple had 3 other children in the years that followed. A daughter, Sarah, born on 12th April 1667 and named after her mother but grief struck when the following year on 17th February 1668 Sarah passed away. Then a son, John, was born heralding in the new year of 1669. To their sorrow he died the following day 2nd January 1669. Summer of 1670 brought the birth on the 11th July of another son, George, to the delight of his parents. Sadly, it was not meant to be and on 31st May 1671 little George died. As sad as this part of their story is it wasn't uncommon in those days. Infant mortality was high, and they still had their first-born son Charles, now a happy and healthy 6-year-old.

Life in the Smithson household carried on as usual. John prepared his sermons, attended meetings and carried out the numerous tasks for a parish priest. Sarah attended to her work amongst their parishioners and cared for their home.

It was now April 1672. John had been the minister for 8 years and life had settled into a routine. It was usual on Saturdays for Rev John Smithson to be pacing the floor of his study, battling with his Sunday sermon. Often he would verbalise his thoughts out loud as he paced. Outside the sun was shining and the occasional sound of children's laughter could be heard through the half open window. His copy of the King James Bible, as well as books of Latin and Greek text, lay open on the smart mahogany desk. John had a guilty secret. In the moulding of his desk was a hidden drawer, where his precious copy of Tyndale's English New Testament as well as various letters and documents lay concealed, away from prying eyes.

Giving a sigh, John sat down heavily in his chair, settling himself before drawing paper and ink towards him with quill in hand he started to write out his sermon.

Sarah, John's wife, was out doing her rounds, visiting the sick and poor of the parish. She came from a well to do family. Her father Rosden was the lessee of the rectory where they lived. A petite lady with dancing brown curls and green sparkling eyes, Sarah liked nothing more than to visit with their parishioners. Mostly they were hard working, interesting people, shop keepers, fishermen and the like, just going about their everyday lives, trying to make ends meet. Although wary in the beginning, her kind, friendly manner had conquered their suspicions and they grew to love her. The children especially, eagerly anticipated her weekly visits, although that might have had something to do with the candy hidden in her basket.

Making her way back along the Elizabethan walls to the rectory Sarah looked out at the horizon with wistful eyes. If you could see with her eyes you might know the sadness that hid behind the smile. How different things would be if only her children had survived. Her relationship with John had become strained lately. Was it because he blamed her or himself in some way for the premature demise of the children? Or was it something else entirely? Whatever it was, it caused a rift between them, that Sarah was at a loss how to bridge.

"John I'm back, Mrs Perkins down Eastern Lane could do with a visit. Their Tommy is very poorly, sadly I don't think he will survive much longer. I'll just start supper now; do you want your meal served in your study or will you join us?"

Without waiting for a reply, Sarah continued her monologue as she made her way to the kitchen. John stayed closeted in his study and Sarah spent the evening alone.

What happened in the early hours of that April Sunday morning no one is quite sure, although there was much speculation at the time. The only person who did know remained forever silent.

John rushed from the house, locking the door behind him, a thing that would never normally happen. Kneeling before the altar, eyes turned heavenward he prayed. As the sound of hushed voices pierced his chaotic thoughts he rose from his knees, the parishioners had begun to arrive. How he got through the service was a miracle in itself. After the singing of a psalm and prayer, he stood up to give his sermon, his eyes looking far away into the distance.

"This morning we will look at the greatest sin 'Thou shalt not kill'. Cain committed murder, killing his brother Abel in cold blood because he was jealous of him." As he continued, his voice got stronger as he vilified those who would go against God's commandments. With beads of sweat standing on his brow he raged on about how God's punishment of hellfire was awaiting anyone who would commit such a heinous crime. His congregation had never heard him speak so eloquently or with so much passion, so much so, that some of the women started to sob openly, some shifted in the pews and all looked uncomfortable.

Suddenly, John was overcome with the emotion of the ordeal and fell backwards in a dead faint. Stunned, the people took what seemed like an age to realise what had happened, before some rushed forward to help him. They carried him reverently to the rectory, but found the door locked. Forcing their way in they stopped, shocked into a stunned silence. John was dropped unceremoniously to the floor. Lying there was his lovely wife Sarah, blood pooled around her with John's walking cane, covered with blood and hair lying beside her.

It all made sense now. The wild eyes, the pallor, and the graphic sermon. John had been referring to himself and the fate that awaited him for his wicked crime. He was immediately arrested and taken to the gaol where he was thrown into the cell. It is recorded that on 2nd May 1672 Leslie Forside refused to watch over him in jail and complained bitterly, using saucy words to express his distaste. At his trial John was asked repeatedly why he had done such a terrible thing. He remained silent and refused to speak of his wife ever again. All eyes were on the judge as he placed the black cover upon his head. His voice was deep and solemn as he pronounced the death sentence. He was to be taken to the place of execution outside the town's walls and hanged by the neck until he was dead.

This was it; the appointed day had arrived. The key grated in the lock as the door was opened with a hard shove.

"Right you, time to go, hurry now, the hangman doesn't like to be kept waiting," the burly gaoler announced.

John straightened up as quickly as his stiff limbs would allow. It would be a relief to get out of this damp cell and be in the fresh air even if it was to be short lived.

Outside he noticed a sturdy chestnut mare waiting, contentedly munching in a nose bag. Attached to her was a rough wooden hurdle.

"Lie down and spread your arms out," commanded the gaoler, as he roughly handled John into place, and secured his arms with ropes.

Outside a large crowd had gathered, eager to see the spectacle. The sun warmed his spread-eagled body, as the horse was led away accompanied by the jeers and taunts of the crowd, his body jarred with every step, as he was dragged up the street towards the Gallows above Tommy the Miller's field.

Mounting the scaffold, John looked out at the large crowd assembled below. It shook him, seeing not even one kind look of sympathy. He could feel the hatred, anger, disappointment and a whole range of other emotions emanating from the crowd that he didn't want to contemplate. Suddenly he felt his knees begin to sag, pulling on the last reserves of his strength he made a determined effort to stand tall for this last time. As the noose was placed around his neck, he could feel the roughness of the rope against his throat. The presiding official asked John if he wished to say any last words. A hush fell upon the crowd as they waited expectantly, surely now at the end he would explain why, if only to clear his conscience before meeting his maker. But no, the people were to be cheated again and left to speculate for all time. John kept his silence to the end. The noose tightened around his neck, and as he hung there twitching, one wonders at what his last thoughts might have been. Regret, remorse, or relief.

John Smithson was taken down and buried in a corner of the churchyard. Why that was allowed no one knows.

Two months after his execution all his worldly goods were appropriated by the Town Guild.

But does no one wonder what happened to his surviving son Charles?

REVENGE IS BITTERSWEET

by Angela Winson

The sun shone on a beautiful June day in 1727 as Margaret Trotter entered St. Cuthbert's Church in her home village of Norham.

Henry, her father, clasped her hand. "It's not too late to change your mind you know." He grinned at his daughter and she knew he was joking.

"I know what I'm doing Dad, John Hackquith is a good man, a respected Burgess and butcher. He will look after me."

"Me and your Mam are proud of you." Henry beamed as he walked his daughter up the aisle.

After they had exchanged vows John turned to his bride and whispered, "Well, Mrs Hackquith, are you ready to fulfil your role as my wife?" He gazed into Margaret's eyes, causing her to blush as she nodded.

Henry Trotter had laid on a befitting spread of food for everyone and when the festivities were over the newlyweds were driven by horse and cart to Berwick upon Tweed by John's grandfather, Robert Weatherburn who had raised him since his own father John, a soldier, had left him in his care when he was a child. Weatherburn, a butcher and a bit of a scoundrel, was convicted of theft in 1711. He was excluded by the Guild but later re-instated and subsequently he took his grandson on as an apprentice butcher.

A year of contented marriage passed and Margaret gave birth to a daughter whom she also named Margaret. All was fine in the Hackquith household but then gradually, and for no particular reason, John's temper was continually on a short fuse and there were days when things were not fine. John gave up the butcher's trade and Margaret was hard pressed to understand why things were going so wrong.

"I thought you enjoyed your job and your standing in the town", she cried, "what has happened to you?"

"What I do or say has nothing to do with you woman!" His words were harsh and stinging as he continued."

"You just look after your child and make my meals and we'll get along fine!" He left the house slamming the door.

Margaret was at a loss as to why he'd turned on her so. He'd taken up drinking and often frequented John and Margaret Ferguson's ale-house where he could buy a pint of beer at any time of the day.

With no trade, there was no money and John was often in debt and at odds with the Guild. As the years rolled by, he was frequently on the wrong side of the law and Margaret was repeatedly on the sharp end of his tongue; sometimes his fists. On one occasion he almost came to blows with a soldier who had helped Margaret remount her horse after a nasty tumble.

"I'll horsewhip you if you lay another finger on my wife!" John's voice rang out across the fields, he raised his whip as if to strike the unfortunate good Samaritan.

"But sir", the soldier began calmly, "I was only aiding the lady to re-mount her horse. I assure you there was no untoward action to warrant a whipping." The soldier stood firm and looked straight into the narrowed eyes of John Hackquith. "Indeed, I would help anyone back onto their horse if they had had the misfortune to tumble.

11

Also, I'm sure you will be relieved to know that your wife has suffered no ill from hers and I will bid you good day." The soldier inclined his head turned sharply and returned to his waiting comrades.

Disgruntled at being dismissed in such a manner John's attention turned to his wife. "Home!" he bellowed turning his horse, and with a sharp lash of the whip across its withers and a kick to its flanks he galloped off in the direction of Berwick.

Back home John Hackquith sat at the kitchen table, anger growing with every passing minute. When Margaret finally appeared, he laid into her unmercifully in an attempt to assuage the humiliation afforded to him by the soldier.

Hearing the screams as she passed the Hackquith's house Margaret Ferguson entered the premises. "What in mercy's name are you doing?" she yelled, "leave her alone!" She tried to pull at his coat but he turned on her.

"Out of my house woman! It's not your business."

"Leave her alone! You'll kill her!"

Hackquith stepped towards her, fist raised. "You leave now before I kill you!"

"You know where I am Margaret, if you need me", she called hurrying out of the door, "I'll be there for you."

Later that day a battered and bruised Margaret sat in the house of Margaret Ferguson. Her wounds were mainly superficial, no bones were broken as John had become adept in knowing just when to stop the beatings to cover up his actions.

"I don't know why you put up with such a man. What gives him the right to think he can beat you and for no justifiable reason after what you've just told me." Margaret Ferguson had cleaned the dried blood from Margaret's forehead. "The man's insane."

"I cannot find an excuse for John's behaviour other than he was raised without a woman's influence."

No sooner were the words out of her mouth when the door crashed open and John strode across the room and beat her again. Fearing for her life and that of Margaret's, Margaret Ferguson threatened to summon the Mayor. Her words had an immediate effect and he left, dragging his wife by the arm up the cobbled street.

For a while, things calmed down in the Hackquith household but days later peace was shattered once again. John's brother, Proston, took Margaret to his house for safety but Hackquith arrived and beat her while she was still in her bed. She was distraught but returned home with John.

The turbulent marriage continued and in 1741 Margaret was saddened by the departure of her now fourteen-year-old daughter.

"To seek a calmer life", she said, after watching her mother suffer at the hands of her father, "I've a position in the big house in Dunbar and I'll try to get back to visit. Take care Mam." Kissing her mother goodbye, she began the long trek north, knowing she may never return or see her mother again.

Margaret endured her life with John with beatings becoming less and less as he drank more and more, staying away for days without explanation.

At 8am one Sunday morning in 1743 he called at the Ferguson's house demanding a pint of beer. The daughter served him as her parents were still in bed. After draining the glass and paying for the beer he left. When Margaret Ferguson came down the stairs, she realised the leather glove, into which she had secreted two pounds fifteen shillings and six pence, was missing.

After questioning her daughter, she went to Hackquith's house to confront him.

"You filthy thief!" she yelled. "You come into my house at a God unearthly hour for beer and steal my money and glove. The Mayor will hear about this!" She turned and moved towards the door but stopped as her glove containing money hit the wall near her.

"Take your damned money", he drawled "and get out of my house."

Margaret picked up the scattered coins and counted them. "There's only two pounds and seven shillings here", re-counting she added, "give me the other eight shillings and six pence."

Hackquith just laughed and slouched further into his chair, clasping his hands behind his head.

This gesture further incensed Margaret. "If I don't have it by tomorrow then it will be the Mayor." Defiantly she marched out of the door.

Not wanting Roger Burnett, the Mayor of Berwick upon Tweed, delving into his underhanded dodgy dealings, he sent William Suddiss, also a Burgess and butcher, to give Margaret Ferguson the remainder of the money.

But Margaret had already been to the Mayor and although he protested his innocence, Hackquith was arrested and taken to the Town Hall Gaol. During his trial Hackquith maintained that he had returned all the money and the glove valued at one penny. Margaret Ferguson claimed that she'd received nothing from the defendant.

William Suddiss could not be found to uphold Hackquith's story. With his fair share of lawbreaking perhaps he was lying low for a while, having kept the eight shillings and six pence for himself.

Maybe Margaret Hackquith saw the arrest as a means of getting revenge for all the years of misery she'd endured at the hands of her husband and in collaboration with Margaret Ferguson had maintained the story of theft. She spoke of the beatings inflicted upon her by her husband but with no proof, it was not added to Hackquith's wrong doing.

Although Hackquith pleaded not guilty to the charge of felony, it was recorded by William Crompton that on November 7th 1743 Roger Burnett, Mayor of Berwick, sentenced the accused to be 'deported to one of His Majesty's Plantations in America and there to remain for seven years'.

On December 17th 1745 John Reavely was instructed to deliver two felons to the keeping of Andrew Reid at His Majesty's Gaol in the County of Surrey in preparation to sail to America.

John Hackquith and Jane Ridpath, who had stood before Roger Burnett, the Mayor, on the same day as Hackquith for stealing from the house of Philip Wilson, began the long journey south. In the lurching prison cart John eyed Jane.

"What was your crime then? Prostitution I'll bet." He tried to move closer but shackles prevented him and he cursed loudly.

Jane shied away from him. "No sir, no." the rusting handcuffs were chaffing her wrists, I … I stole a gown and some lucifer's." She lowered her eyes, not wanting to strike a conversation with such a vile man.

"How much were they worth then? A pretty penny if you're off to America?"

"The gown was four shillings and eleven pennies, the lucifer's one penny."

Hackquith sneered. "What a piffling amount. If you're intent on stealing at least make it worth the sentencing. Did you plead benefit of the clergy or are you illiterate?" Hackquith himself had pleaded so but had failed to obtain leniency.

"I am educated sir and I did plead benefit of the clergy but to no avail and I do not wish to further our conversation." She turned away from the now glowering Hackquith.

"Have it your way missy but the hot-blooded Americans will soon crush your 'mightier than thou' attitude." He laughed knowingly, "Oh yes missy, crush."

The journey to Surrey, by both cart and coal ship, left Hackquith and Ridpath fraught and exhausted. Soon it was time to board the ship that was to be their home for the next few weeks. Coming from Northumberland Hackquith had no knowledge of where he was or what docks he, along with hundreds more convicts, had been herded onto before boarding the ship bound for America.

Handcuffed and shackled he portrayed a broken man as he was pushed and shoved along the wooden deck towards the steps that led down to the belly of the creaking wooden ship as it rolled on the tide, eager to embrace the wide-open seas. Stumbling, Hackquith caught a glimpse of Jane Ridpath, her hair matted and clothes torn as she was dragged towards another set of steps. This was it. Their fate was sealed, to serve seven years working on a plantation somewhere in America – he didn't even know his destination once he'd crossed the Atlantic or whether he and Jane Ridpath would ever cross paths again.

Back in Berwick upon Tweed, Margaret Hackquith had no regrets or second thoughts about not defending her husband and certainly didn't miss the constant beatings he gave her.

Left to fend for herself, Margaret had to do whatever she could in order to survive. Unfortunately, she often found herself on the wrong side of the law for reportedly keeping a 'disorderly house' by allowing prostitutes to lodge there - although nothing was ever proven.

ESCAPE!

by E.P.Mack

"On this day 22nd April 1787, the accused Peter Gentle has been found guilty of larceny."

He could not believe his ears! How could that be right? Was this justice? He glared at the gaffer willing him to look up at him in shame or apology but the man deliberately looked away. How could he lie like that? He knew perfectly well that he had given the oats to Peter in payment for moving all that extra barley.

The owners of the brewery, Burnett Roger Grieve and James Begbie, had caught Peter giving the four forpets of oats to Marjery Thompson and had challenged him. He explained about the arrangement with the gaffer but that wicked man had denied it outright, knowing he would lose his job for giving any unauthorised payment, and especially for something he should have done himself. Of course, the owners had taken Peter Gentle to court - who would believe a black man, working class, and former slave when their respected white gaffer said otherwise. Peter's heart raced and his head thumped, the room swirled around him. He thought he would pass out. He looked across at Sarah who was quietly crying. He almost missed the sentence he was given:

He was "to be transported beyond the sea for seven years". He heard a gasp and realised it came from him. Sarah sobbed loudly.

So far away for so long! And how could he bear having his freedom taken from him again? Peter had been enslaved as a young boy and had only been given his freedom a few years ago when Lady Hanwell, believing that it was against her Christian faith to make slaves of any children of God, had given them all legal papers setting them free. Most of them stayed on the estate as paid workers but Peter, now nearing fifty, had decided to leave. He had travelled as far as Berwick upon Tweed where, with his broad shoulders and strong arms he had easily got a job as a malt man at one of the many breweries in the town. He had married a widow who had two boys, and he was very happy. Now all that was to be taken away from him! And how would Sarah manage without him there to support and protect them? A dark despair clutched at him.

He tried to concentrate on what else they were saying: He was "to be conveyed back to the prison from whence he came and to be conveyed from thence to the public hulks upon the River Thames or to such other place as His Majesty shall appoint for receiving convicts for transportation." (America was no longer accepting convicts from England so they were going to be sent to Australia instead.)

Escape!

Even further away and everyone knew the conditions on the convict ships were so bad that many of the prisoners died on the journey. If he even got there safely, he would never be able to come back to his family. It was all so unjust and there was absolutely nothing he could do about it!..............Or was there?

His mind working furiously, when he said goodbye to Sarah, he whispered, "Get me a file!"

She looked startled but when she came to the prison with his meal that evening and handed it to the gaoler to pass through to Peter, she said emphatically, "Be careful that stew's hot!"

Peter took a mouthful and found the small piece of a file hidden under the vegetables. How could he hide it with the grim-faced gaoler looking on? Suddenly he coughed and spat into the corner of the dirt floor.

"Oh Sarah" he moaned, "I nearly swallowed that stone" and quickly kicked dirt over the file.

"You should count yourself lucky to have any food," muttered the gaoler, "You don't deserve it!"

Sarah had to leave then and the gaoler went to check on his other charges. Peter took the opportunity to transfer the file to a tiny hole in the waistband of his old velveret breeches.

He had to try to escape. He did not know when he would be sent to London and it would take a long time to get through any of the iron bars of his cell. But it became apparent that the prison keeper Mr Dickinson went to work in his public house every evening, leaving a beadle in charge. The beadle usually fell asleep so they were not well supervised after dark.

Peter filed furiously every night, all night. His fingers soon became bruised and bloody as the file wore down but he did not stop. Every few weeks Sarah brought another piece of file hidden in his evening meal. He planned to cut through the bottom of two bars and then bend them out of the way, so that he could squeeze through. Fortunately the cells were at street level and had no window glass, only bars - not so good when it rained in but a blessing for anyone trying to get out! Every morning he covered over the telltale shiny marks on the bars with dirt from the floor and lay down on his pallet to sleep. His gaolers got used to him sleeping a lot and as he caused no trouble they left him alone, suspecting nothing.

 It was 21st October before he had managed to cut right through the second bar and he knew he had to go straight away before anyone noticed what he had done. He could not even say goodbye to Sarah.

The bars were much harder to bend than he had hoped and he was soon sweating and panicking but then suddenly the last bar gave way and he had a gap big enough to put his head through. If the beadle happened to come along he was done for - he had to get out NOW!

Escape!

He was glad he had lost weight while he was in prison or he would never have squeezed through the gap but taking off his thick coat he could just manage it. No-one came shouting or rushing after him and, heart in his mouth, he was soon flitting between the shadows down Hide Hill and Sandgate and through the town walls to the Quayside.

The main salmon trade had finished for the year only the week before but there were still several smacks tied up, loaded with grain, or eggs, and some with fish swimming in the wells in the bottom of the smack. They were ready for the high tide that would allow them through the channel and out to sea. Only one or two still had their gangplanks down. Peter watched from the shadows, sweat trickling down his back, heart thudding so loudly he thought someone must hear! At last the watchman from the "Swiftly Susie "went over to the other side of the boat to relieve himself into the river, Peter strode up the gangplank as if he belonged there, and quickly cowered down among the boxes and barrels. The smack set sail minutes later, before anyone from the prison even started to search for him. He hoped that if he was discovered on the voyage the skipper would let him work his passage to London, not knowing that he had an escaped convict on board!

The crew found him soon after leaving Berwick and to his horror the skipper threatened to throw him in leg irons. However, being a practical man and always needing an extra pair of hands, he allowed him to work instead. Peter's little finger on his left hand was permanently contracted up and was soon aching as he pulled on the ropes but he worked so hard that when they docked in London he was offered paid work. Peter declined - he had to get away from any links to Berwick. He hurried down towards the big warehouses and in a dark corner he fell into a deep asleep. No-one came looking for him, and next morning, not quite believing that he was really free, he walked along the river to a different dock and got taken on to unload a precious cargo of tea. No-one commented on his black skin for there were many free black men around. They did comment that he was a hard worker and he soon became a regular on the docks.

After two years he was able to send money to his beloved Sarah so that she and the boys could join him in London.

Sarah told him about the "Wanted" notices in all the newspapers - the "Kelso", two Newcastle and three Edinburgh papers, as well as in the "Hue and Cry". Peter was amazed to hear that there was a reward of ten guineas for whoever caught him.

"Eee, I wouldna ha thought I were worth that much!" he joked, in his adopted dialect.

"Eee, more than that pet." declared Sarah, hugging him.

Treason for a Sixpence

by Homer Lindsay

Events in Berwick-upon-Tweed in 1816 took a dark turn, when a sentence of death was passed upon five people.

The British Gazette and Berwick Advertiser, in its 10th February edition, reported that 'On Thursday night, were apprehended in this town, a gang of coiners (all Irish), consisting of 2 men, 3 women, a boy and girl with all the implements of their nefarious traffic. Yesterday they underwent an examination before the Magistrates and were committed for trial.'

It all started when Mary Anderson, who ran a lodging house in Walkergate Lane, let two beds in her upstairs room on Sunday 4th February 1816 to Barnard Duffey, his wife Margaret and Maria Courtney. The following day, James and Mary Moen joined them to occupy a third bed.

Mary did not like the look of them but could not afford to turn business away.

Parish constable, Thomas Hope, enjoyed the company of the widow, Mary Anderson. When doing his official duty rounds of the town's lodging houses he always came last to Walkergate Lane hoping to spend time with her.

On Wednesday 7th February, Mary expressed her disquiet to Thomas about her upstairs lodgers, so he went up to speak to them. He came upon a man using scissors to cut a small round piece from a thin sheet of copper. The man quickly concealed the implements behind his back.

"What are you doing?" asked the constable.

"Nothing" he replied.

Thomas looked at the group of two men and three women asking their names.

"Barnard Duffey" said the man with the scissors.

"James Moen" said the other.

Margaret Duffey, Maria Courtney and Mary Moen replied in turn.

The constable decided to let it go for now but would keep an eye on these lodgers; he wanted to be sure that Mary Anderson would be safe.

The following evening Constable Hope told local men William White and Joseph Park of his suspicions and asked them to check the back of the lodging house for any indications of wrongdoing; he was going to see Mary.

The top room could be observed from an old wall behind the lodging house. William and Joseph saw three women sitting around a table near the window. A burning candle was between them. Two men were behind them, facing outward. The observers could see Margaret Duffey and Mary Moen cutting round pieces from copper with scissors. Maria Courtney would take each one and pass it to James Moen, who dipped them in a small pot. They came out silver in colour. Courtney took them back, rubbed them between finger and thumb and put them in a cup held by Barnard Duffey. The observers saw this happen several times, like it was a process.

"What are they doing," whispered Joseph.

"If I'm not mistaken, they are coining," replied William.

They continued to watch until they saw Mary and Maria leave the house. They followed the women to the grocer's shop in Castlegate. Moen went inside while Courtney remained at the door.

The woman asked Isabella Johnson, the shopkeeper, for tea, sugar, bread and tobacco, paying with two sixpence coins. Accepting her change, she left the shop.

William had observed the transaction through the window and now entered the shop, asking Isabella, "Let me see the coins she used to pay you."

Isabella showed him the two sixpences and said, "What's wrong?"

"Keep these apart from all other money, Isabella," William muttered while marking them, "I think they are counterfeit. I'll be right back."

He and Park ran after the two women, detaining them on the corner of Castlegate and Walkergate Lane.

Joseph went to report to the Mayor while William returned to the grocer's shop with Moen and Courtney.

"How did this woman pay for these purchases" asked William, indicating Mary Moen.

"With these two coins" Isabella replied, holding them up for inspection.

Moen desperately shouted, "They are not the coins I gave you; you must have received them from someone else!"

Isabella confirmed that these were the only coins in the cup she had placed them in.

William White apprehended the two miscreants and took them back to the lodging house.

Meanwhile, Mayor Christopher Cookson, having heard the report from Joseph Park, ordered Thomas Hope, Charles Ferguson and four other constables to accompany him to the lodging house. When they arrived they rushed upstairs, leaving Ferguson and Park to guard the entrance.

A man tried to leave the building but Park stopped him, telling him to go into the lower room.

Elizabeth Ormston, visiting her mother Mary, whispered, "That man is the leader of the gang upstairs."

In the upstairs room, Thomas Hope detained Courtney, Duffey and the Moens while they and the room were searched. A pair of scissors, a small empty glass phial and a pocket book with a copper door-plate was found on Mary Duffey.

On James Moen they found a quantity of white powder, which he claimed was starch.

A file, the teeth of which were full of copper shavings, was found on the mantlepiece. In a corner of the room there were three round pieces of copper, coloured to resemble sixpences; nine more were polished; three cut and rounded; and a cup containing a silver substance.

Another pair of scissors were on the table and some clippings of copper on the floor; the edges of the scissors were tinged with copper.

"I think we have here all the evidence we need to prove counterfeiting" said the Mayor, "let's take them in."

As they descended the stairs, Constable Hope went into the lower room to apprehend the leader of the gang, Barnard Duffey.

"He's not here!" shouted Thomas, "He's escaped! He must have climbed through the window."

The remaining four were taken into custody to be held at the Gaol.

It later transpired that on that same night, a girl came into Ann Wilson's shop, a dealer in spirits, and paid 6d for a pot of whisky, which she took away in a teacup. A few minutes later another pot of whisky was requested by a boy carrying the same teacup, who paid with another sixpence. Ann disliked the look of the coin, returned it and refused to serve the boy.

The absconder, Barnard Duffey, was later arrested and confined to the House of Correction in Hexham on a charge of assaulting a poor woman who had been travelling with him.

He was later identified as one of the gang of coiners and escorted back to Berwick to be imprisoned with the others.

The case came before the Berwick Court of Sessions on 24th July 1816.

The indictment read that '..not having the fear of God before their eyes but being moved and seduced by the instigation of the Devil and contriving and intending our said Lord the King and his People craftily, deceitfully, feloniously and traitorously to deceive and defraud on the Eighth day of February in the fifty-sixth year of the Reign of our Sovereign Lord George the Third, with force and arms at the Parish of Berwick-upon-Tweed, did forge, counterfeit and coin, to the likeness and similitude of the good, legal and current Money and Silver Coin of the Realm called a sixpence.'

The charge was one of high treason. Also indicted were John Duffey and Ann Courtney, the boy and girl. However, the Grand Jury did not find a true bill against them and they were discharged.

The owner of the British Gazette and Berwick Advertiser, Mr Hugo Richardson, paid great attention to the case because he was concerned that as a treasonable offence this gang were likely to be sentenced to death if, as seemed likely, they were found guilty. He had joined with penal reformers around the country who, from 1810, were condemning English criminal law as a *'bloody code, a monolithic mass of draconian statutes inherited from a former, less civilised age.'* [1]

The newspaper frequently published new perspectives on this penal reform debate.

None of this helped the five accused who had pleaded not guilty, but who could offer no defence in contradiction of the numerous witnesses who testified against them.

The Recorder, Mr Christopher Cookson, summarised the facts of the case to the jury. They did not take long to come to a verdict of "Guilty."

Mr Cookson, in a most impressive and affecting manner, then pronounced sentence, "James Moen, Mary Moen, Barnard Duffey, Margaret Duffey and Maria Courtney, you have been found guilty of high treason and I pronounce that you be taken from hence to the place from whence you came and from thence be drawn on a Hurdle to the place of execution and there be hanged by the neck until your bodies be dead."

There was uproar in the courtroom.

The five defendants rose in shock and despair, frantically pleading for mercy.

Chaos reigned as spectators were seen to cry, shout in disbelief or raise their fists in defiance of the sentence.

"A punishment is certainly justified but they surely do not deserve the death penalty" cried Mary Anderson to Thomas Hope, "they only tried to pass two shillings worth of forged coins. Three of them are no more than 23 years of age!"

Thomas replied, "Well, that is the law of the land, Mary."

The British Gazette and Berwick Advertiser reported the court case and outcome on Saturday 27th July and in a separate editorial reflected on the outrage expressed by the 'good people of Berwick' at capital punishment for forgery.

Mary Moen, languishing in Berwick gaol, gave birth to a son on 5th August 1816 who was christened James in the Roman Catholic chapel of Berwick three days later. He was never to see his mother again.

Whether it was the local newspaper or the wider penal reform campaign that influenced matters, it was on the 13th August 1816, just 11 days before the scheduled day of execution, that the Prince Regent granted a royal pardon to the five, conditional upon them being transported to the coast of New South Wales for the rest of their respective natural lives.

James Moen and Barnard Duffey arrived on board the 'Justitia' off Woolwich on 10th October 1816 and remained on the hulk until they were transferred to a convict transport on 20th November 1816. They set sail for Australia aboard the 'Shipley' on 20th December, arriving in Sydney on 24th April 1817.

Mary Moen, Margaret Duffey and Maria Courtney sailed for Sydney aboard the 'Friendship' in June 1817 with another 98 convicts, disembarking in New South Wales on 14th January 1818.

Meanwhile, life in Berwick-upon-Tweed settled down after the traumatic events of 1816; Mary Anderson's friendship with Thomas Hope continued to flourish and they set a date for marriage in late 1817.

The overwhelmingly negative image of this 'Bloody code' underpinned the dramatic and unexpected repeal of the capital statutes in the 1830's and survived to define a whole era of criminal justice history.[1]

Acknowledgements :

[1] HANDLER, P. (2005). FORGERY AND THE END OF THE 'BLOODY CODE' IN EARLY NINETEENTH-CENTURY ENGLAND. The Historical Journal, 48(3), 683-702. doi:10.1017/S0018246X05004620 - reproduced with permission.

© National Maritime Museum

A Fortunate Man

by Veronica Burningham

Well, I made it. There were plenty of times I doubted that I would but here I am. My name is Thomas Green, I've just turned 18, and I can't blame anyone but myself for what I have been through.

Perhaps I should have stayed in Glasgow where I had a decent job as a house painter. I had a good family too. My mother taught in a little school and she made sure I learned to read and write. Trouble is, I've always been easily led, and when my friend Jimmy said he was going to join the Army I thought a change would be good, and that's how I became a Private in the 25th Regiment. I knew straight away it was a mistake, with the marching, discipline and being shouted at all the time.

That's when the thieving started. Jimmy persuaded me that it was easy and we could make some money. Life with Jimmy was sort of exciting, and I have to confess I enjoyed the thrill of getting away with something, though of course I didn't in the end.

I was pretty stupid then, 17 years old and charged with stealing a silver pocket watch worth ten shillings from Mr. James Hawthorn at the Kings Arms in Berwick. That was on 27th December 1815. They could have charged me with two more watches at ten shillings each from Mr. Charles

Mowat and Mr. Robert Fluker, but it seems the one was enough to convict me. I offered Mr. Hawthorn's watch to a pedlar and that's when I got caught.

It was horrible standing in the dock on 17th January 1816, seeing the sea of faces looking back at me and gripping the rail hard to try and stop shaking. They say there were 1000 people there, though I don't know why my trial was so popular. You'd think they would have better things to do. I found if I turned slightly to the left, my blind right eye shut out a lot of the courtroom, which felt a bit better.

I pleaded not guilty but, as I'd been caught red-handed, it wasn't anything more than defiance really. I was found guilty of grand larceny and sentenced to seven years transportation. At the time I couldn't even begin to imagine what that really meant. I felt such shame, especially when I said I didn't know where the watches were. Later, in gaol, the feeling got the better of me and I told the gaoler where to find them. Trouble was, there were 18 of them

I was sent back to gaol with quite a few others, waiting to be sent to London to be put on the convict ship. The trip down there wasn't too bad, the master was a fair man and the sea was calm.

The hulks were a very different matter. These were mostly decommissioned warships, stripped of their masts, sails and rigging. Someone in prison in Berwick had said we wouldn't be transported straight away but put in the hulks on the river at Woolwich until there were enough of us to fill the convict ship. I found out a lot about them in the three months I was there. About 1776, a man called Duncan Campbell, who had been involved in the slave trade, and then with transportation to America, bought two hulks, the Justitia, which was 260 tons, and the Censor, an ex-frigate. He stripped them and added penthouses on the decks to house the prisoners. Many of the inmates were kept out on the decks, some having no shoes, stockings or shirts.

Campbell was put in charge of ballasting the banks of the river to make secure moorings for the hulks. The convicts were used as hard labour to do this work, tied in gangs and wearing shackles. The public used to come to watch the poor wretches toiling on the banks without proper clothes or shoes against the weather. In the first two years 176 out of 632 prisoners died. By the time I got there things had improved a bit.

We were used as labour for the shipyards and were subject to naval rather than penal law. We mostly wore uniforms to distinguish us from the regular shipyard workers. The worst part were the shackles which we had to wear all the time we were working in the gangs. You had to lift your leg quite high to walk and it was tiring. If you committed an offence your shackle might be made heavier or you would have one on each leg. People often had a sort of tic for ages after removal of the irons, still high stepping as if they were wearing them.

We were woken at 5am. We washed, ate breakfast and scrubbed the decks before being marched off to the shipyard for hard labour, such as unloading ballast from ships, dredging channels or moving rubble. A lot of the work was dangerous and there were many accidents, as well as some deaths. It was then back to the hulk for lunch and another shift in the shipyard until 5.30pm. After supper we were expected to join in prayers and the illiterate were taught to read and write. Bed was at 8pm when the hatches were locked down.

Transportation was big business. Some years later I learnt that altogether 825 convict ships sailed to Australia, with about 200 per ship. The ships' masters had mostly been slaving contractors and were paid £17.17s.6d for each convict, to cover clothing, food and passage, whether they arrived dead or alive. The unscrupulous amongst them would pocket some of the money so the convicts had even less to eat and wear.

The ships were converted merchantmen, usually with two rows of berths against the hull, one above the other, with a central corridor between them. Each berth was six feet square with headroom of usually less than six feet and housed four convicts. I was lucky, being only 5 feet 5 inches I could at least stand upright. Hatches were secured at night. When it was hot it was unbearable, and the pitch in the seams melted and burned those it fell on. In rough weather, the berths got soaked with sea water and we lay on saturated bedding, often very cold. The total darkness was an added horror.

We were given two pints of stinking, warm water per day. The main food was brined beef, which we called 'salt horse'. We were half-starved, often ill. Quite a few died and were unceremoniously dumped over the side. If one of our number died, we tried to conceal the fact for as long as possible, so we got their rations. The only good thing was that our irons were removed once we were on the open sea.

On 6th May 1816 I was put on the convict ship, "Mariner", together with 145 others. When I went it could take up to 252 days to get to Botany Bay, of which around 10 weeks were spent in port, doing repairs and taking on supplies. We didn't go directly to Australia because sailing ships had to go with the prevailing winds, so we went via South America.

I had decided while on the hulks that I was going to survive and overcome whatever lay ahead of me. That was when I grew up. At the time I had little idea of the horrors of the convict ship, with its stench and illness, and being covered with filth, vomit and other indescribable horrors, most of the way. When we got to Botany Bay, it was 11th October. I heard later that by 1830 the journey time had come down to 110 days.

So here I am. The ship has docked and our shackles have been put back on. Most of us have been brought up on deck ready for disembarkation. The scene on the docks is amazing. After six months shut in a berth with three others, there are more people than you can possibly count, all busy. Lines of convicts in shackles are loading and unloading ships, horse-drawn carriages are coming and going collecting and delivering parcels and other goods. The noise is indescribable, especially to someone who for six months has only heard moans and whimpers and a bit of conversation, along with the noises of a ship on the high seas.

As I stood there on the deck, I thought back to my old life, and then something inside me changed. I had to serve seven years, possibly hard labour, but I was going to survive and learn. When it was over I was going to make something of myself in this new and strange land.

A Fortunate Life

by Veronica Burningham

 I'm 81 years old today and sitting on the verandah looking over the garden which my wife, Rosie, planted when we first moved here. We've just finished my birthday lunch, and I can hear the women in the kitchen chattering and laughing as they clear away and wash up.

I find myself looking backwards more these days and thinking about how I got here. I remember so clearly landing at Botany Bay and thinking 'Here I am, Thomas Green, 18 years old and setting foot in Australia, the other side of the world from where I was born.' It's odd but I was actually quite excited. It was late afternoon and we had just been marched down the gangplank of the sailing ship, Mariner, and were standing on dry land for the first time in many months. It felt as though it was swaying under my feet and it took a couple of days for that feeling to go away.

By 1816 when I arrived, as a convict transported for seven years, Sydney had grown from a small village into a sizeable town. Buildings were made of timber and stone, with only a few of the original wattle and daub ones still in use. It was strange and very different to what we had been accustomed to. In summer, which was the season we were coming into when we arrived in October, the heat was well-nigh unbearable, and was often followed by torrential rain and huge thunderstorms. The wildlife was odd too. The birds included kookaburras, as well as brightly coloured parrots and cockatoos. Kangaroos, echidnas, wombats and goannas roamed the scrubby bush surrounding the town, along with a variety of snakes.

It was such a huge change from the last nine months that it took a long time to adjust. Gone were the dreadful bunks on the Mariner, where we either sweltered or shivered. Gone were the black nights, hunger and over-crowding. Even better, the prison hulks on the river Thames in London, with their shackles, hard labour and cruel overseers, were just a bad memory.

Most convicts lived in two-or three-room houses which they shared with other convicts or a family, in an area called The Rocks, which had a pretty rough and disreputable reputation. We had a table and chairs, crockery, cutlery, a stove and a bed. We were able to wash our clothes and hang them in the sun to dry.

We had to collect our food rations from the government store. The daily ration per person was 1 pound of beef or pork, 1 pound of corn (sometimes still on the cob) and 1 pound of wheat flour to make bread.

The meat would sometimes be rotten because it had been on a ship for months or even years before arriving. If the weather was bad and the crops damaged, we were given less to eat. Women and teenagers got smaller rations than the men so were often hungry.

If you were lucky enough to have a garden you could grow food to supplement your rations, and if there was a surplus you could sell it. Vegetables grow really fast here and I soon had quite a market garden going. I teamed up with Sam, who had served his time and was now an established trader in The Rocks, and he sold all that I could grow. This provided a welcome extra income, which I saved towards the day I would have served my sentence.

I met my wife, Rosie, through my gardening. She lived in the house next door and often came to help with the weeding, or to just sit in the sun and talk to me while I worked. She had been transported at around the same time as me, but from Portsmouth. She lived with her family in that city, and had stolen some vegetables from a garden to help feed her younger siblings. I think she enjoyed the irony of helping to tend the produce instead of stealing it. Her sentence finished a bit before mine but she stayed in The Rocks until I was free to leave. We were married when I took up my first land allocation, and she came with me and Jake when we moved to the Hawkesbury River.

Work for us convicts started at 7am. We were given work clothes, called 'slops', by the government. These consisted of a cotton shirt, a blue woollen jacket, a waistcoat, white trousers, shoes, and a woollen cap or hat. Most of us worked in government 'gangs' doing many different jobs. We cut down trees, made bricks and houses, and built doors, windows and furniture. Other heavy work involved pulling carts and moving barrels of water. The government lumberyard, on the corner of Bridge and George streets, was where men with trades worked. Carpenters, wheelwrights, tailors, and blacksmiths made chains and work tools.

I worked at tree cutting for a while but then I had a stroke of luck. I was helping someone write a letter home when a government clerk happened to walk by. He stopped and asked me how well I could read and write and said that I should go with him to his superior as they were looking for people to work in the government offices. The result was that I served my term in relative comfort.

When the day's work was done we were free to take other work to make some money. I did various things, from a bit of painting, which was my trade in Glasgow, to standing in for clerks who were ill, or when the office was short-staffed. I saved as much as possible, even denying myself extra food when I had the chance to buy some because I had a plan.   I had heard about the land that was being granted to army officers and some expirees and I was determined to apply as soon as I was free. Along with the money from the market garden I managed to save quite a tidy sum

Not all convicts were so lucky. Those sent to Norfolk Island or Van Diemen's Land had a much worse time, with harsh overseers. Beatings were common and the cat o' nine tails was a popular punishment with the authorities. Those on the mainland who committed crimes or were lazy were often transferred to one of these places as a punishment, which of course acted as quite a deterrent to most of us.

If you worked hard and behaved well you could get a Ticket-of-Leave. This meant you could work for yourself provided you stayed in a specified area, reported regularly to the local authorities, and went to church every Sunday. You couldn't leave the colony.

Once you had served your term you were issued with a Certificate of Freedom, proving you were a free man and could travel anywhere, even returning to England if you could afford it.

I had two more strokes of luck. In 1792 Captain Arthur Phillip stepped down as Governor and returned to England. Major Francis Grose took over as Acting Governor and proved himself to be much less harsh. He increased the food rations and also allowed expirees to take up land. This had previously only been granted to army officers and immigrants who arrived of their own accord, rather than being transported as convicts.

I applied for, and was granted, 100 acres, which I took up on the Hawksbury River, a fertile district to the north and west of Sydney. The government also provided two years supplies until the land could be cleared and put under cultivation. I was lucky again in that I had made friends with a farm worker from the north of England, whose term expired at the same time as mine. He came in with me and taught me all I know about farming. Jake Conners has been my best friend ever since, and he now owns an adjacent property.

Over the next few years, Jake and I improved the land, built a house, planted crops and then bought a few sheep to graze land not suited to cultivation. We also bought adjacent land when it became available, and ended up with over 1000 acres. The area was getting pretty crowded with soldier settlers and expirees, especially as it was fairly close to Sydney, which was now a thriving city.

In 1815 a road had been built across the Blue Mountains, west of Sydney. This led to a huge area of grassland being opened up for settlement and was ideal for sheep and cattle. In 1835 Jake and I sold up all our holdings on the Hawkesbury River and moved our families and stock to a large holding about 200 miles west of Bathurst. This town was founded in 1815 and named after Henry Bathurst, 3rd Earl of Bathhurst, who was the Secretary for War and the Colonies. It was one of the first settlements west of the Great Dividing Range. Gold was discovered nearby in 1851 and the population grew rapidly.

We moved at just the right time and, once settled, concentrated on raising sheep for which the country was ideal. The demand for meat from the growing population continued to grow to the point where we could hardly keep up.

Eventually we divided up the land so we each had identical holdings. We built houses and our wives planted gardens. Life was good and, as large landholders, we were admitted into the top echelons of Bathurst society. We now run about 50,000 sheep and 1000 cattle. Our holdings are no longer measured in acres but in square miles, 70000 between us.

As founder members of many of the institutions that have grown up in and around Bathurst, both Jake and I are kept busy sitting on various committees and helping to run various organisations. I was instrumental in helping to set up the school as I feel very strongly that education is important, not just for the learning side of things, but because it provides a firm foundation for the future and helps to keep people out of the sort of trouble I got into back in England.

We employ a large number of stockmen, many of whom are Aboriginals. Their race has had a really bad time since the white men arrived. In many places their numbers have been decimated and their food sources have disappeared. They are excellent horsemen and natural stockmen. They are the ones who break in the brumbies (wild horses) that we catch to use as saddle horses, and they seem to have no fear. They are wonderful trackers and happy to stay out for weeks, sometimes months, at a time, maintaining fences and checking on stock.

I used to go on the big droves when we took sheep or cattle down the stock routes for sale in the towns and cities, but these days I leave it to the younger generation. I have four healthy sons who run the station now, and two daughters who are married to nearby graziers, so I still see them often.

I miss the old days, especially the droving. There is a special kind of comradeship on the stock trails and, in my opinion, there is nothing in the world as good as sitting round a camp fire at the end of a long day. This is when we exchange stories and make plans. I found it hard to give up the running of the station to the boys, but feel blessed that all four of them wanted to carry on the family business. So many of the young people just want to get off the land and into the cities for a more exciting life.

My youngest son, Jack, is the most entrepreneurial. He has bought a woollen mill so we can spin our own yarn which adds value to the wool clip. A lot of it goes to various armies for greatcoats. Merino wool is also much sought after by the clothing trade, especially as the cities are growing and people have more time and money to spend on social occasions.

The two oldest boys, Thomas Junior and Frank, are the true stockmen, looking after the flocks and the land. Of course, that means they are often away from home for long periods of time, and I do sometimes get to be a bit 'hands on' while they're away. I have to be careful not to tread on anyone's toes though. It is quite difficult letting go of the reins of something you love, especially when you are still living your life in the midst of it.

George is the horseman, and he is in charge of the Aboriginal stockmen and the provision of good stock horses. He is nearly as good a horseman as the Aboriginals, and has a gentle way with the horses which they respect. He has also expanded his side of the business a bit. Lots of city-dwellers are keen to get out into the bush and experience life as it was for the first settlers. He takes small groups trekking and camping, and also runs horse management courses, which is a very new thing in these parts. He has hit on a great idea as the demand for these courses is growing all the time.

I often think that the women are the unsung heroes of our way of life. A sheep station is like a small town, and it is the women who make sure everything runs smoothly, that we always have enough food and other supplies, and who see that all the hands are looked after. They act as teachers, nurses and cooks, amongst other things, and in general hold it all together. From the sounds coming from the kitchen, I think the clearing up is almost finished, and I can hear them sending the children off to play so the grown-ups can have a bit of time to relax.

Now I sit here waiting for them all to join me. I can see Jake coming out of the house to sit with me and discuss plans for the next season. We have come such a long way from being convicts and I see now that transportation was the best thing that ever happened to me. Without it I certainly wouldn't have what I have now, and would probably be living in a hovel in Berwick or Glasgow, ekeing out a living as a house painter and worrying about where the next meal was coming from. I thank God often for my good fortune.

THE CONSTABLE'S TALE

by E.P.Mack

I was proud to be a member of the new police force, with my smart blue uniform and tall black hat, but I must admit I did not like this part of the job. Officially, the stocks had not been in use since 1849 but Grace Guthrie could not pay the fine for being drunk and disorderly so she was being publicly humiliated in the stocks. In this same year 1856, she had already spent 4 months in the House of Correction. She was only 25, a pretty little thing with golden curls and sparkling blue eyes - though I suspect it was unshed tears making them sparkle today. Well, like it or not, a constable's job is to keep the peace and uphold the law, so I sat her down on the low bench outside the town hall and stretched out her legs to rest her ankles on the lower bar of the stocks There was room for three criminals in the stocks, but that day it was only Grace Guthrie. She began to cry. I snapped the upper bar down and locked it in place. Her feet were so tiny she could probably have squeezed them through the holes and walked away, but she seemed resigned to her fate and just sat head bowed, tears running down her cheeks while she waited for a crowd to gather and the rotten food to be thrown. I stood nearby - in the past young ruffians had been known to hide stones in the stuff they were throwing and that could be dangerous. I couldn't allow that. I think we were both surprised when nothing happened. A few people even shouted support

"Keep your chin up Gracie," and "It'll soon be over love" and to me, "You big bully!"

But most of the good citizens of Berwick, I think, were embarrassed to witness this medieval punishment and went round the other side of the town hall shaking their heads. The businesspeople and the Freemen wanted drunkenness punished but the ordinary people just seemed sorry for her - probably remembered times when they themselves had had too much beer and had been a bit noisy going home.

Over the next several years Grace Guthrie was often in court - always for being drunk and disorderly. She was never sent to the stocks again but to the common jail or more often to the workhouse. One day, walking her up the alley in Featherbed Lane to the workhouse once again, I asked her,

"Why do you drink so much and make your life so miserable? The workhouse can't be much fun!"

"No, it isn't," she smiled sadly, "Cleaning, cooking, washing clothes and picking oakum," a pause, and a chuckle, "but the food is great - gruel, bread and cheese , sometimes a bit of meat or fish - what more could anyone want! It doesn't matter anyway," she sighed, "My life is always miserable, but having a drink helps to numb the pain".

"What pain is that?" I asked but she turned away and did not answer.

It was later one of the pub landlords told me the rumours:

Grace came from a respectable family - her father was a shoemaker, and both parents staunch Presbyterians. The rumours said that when Grace was fifteen, she and her mother went up to Scotland to stay with relatives for Mrs Guthrie to have her expected baby. They stayed for four months and came home with a baby girl. But the gossips speculated that the baby brought back from Scotland was really Grace's baby, the offspring of an unscrupulous relative who had been staying with them. Whether or not, its true that when they came back, Grace was packed off into service in one of the big houses.

Less than a year later, Grace was pregnant to the son of the family she was working for. Back to Scotland she went with her mother and her mother had another baby girl to look after. Don't take any of this as the absolute truth - its only what people say. But something must have caused her to take refuge in drink, don't you think? Why do I listen to gossip? Well, as a town constable I do need to know what's going on in the town, and besides, Grace's misfortunes somehow bothered me.

When she came back to Berwick, Grace had been dismissed from the place where she had been working, and worse, her parents disowned her and banned her from the house. I know it's not for me to judge but I thought that was a bit harsh. Anyway, apart from an odd night or two with one of her friends, she found herself on the streets. She began seeking solace and shelter in the local public houses. There were plenty of them to welcome her - about fifty at that time. From there it had been a short, inevitable step to the courts and punishment.

I got to know Grace Guthrie a little too well as the years went by. She often created havoc on the streets, scandalising the upright residents of Berwick with her drunken shouting, her raucous laughter and her enthusiastic renditions of the bawdy songs from the public houses. I never knew her to be nasty in her drunkenness. Her friends said she was "good fun" and "a laugh" and they all seemed very fond of her. I suppose from having witnessed her distress in the stocks, I had a soft spot for her myself.

One good thing happened to Grace in 1862 - to everyone's surprise, she got married.

John White - or Wight as it is sometimes written - was a hard-working labourer. He had lived in Shaws Lane most of his life, but unlike most of the residents there he was never in trouble with the police. In fact, I often used to pass the time of day with him when he came up Hide Hill from work. He used to have a drink or two (or more!) with Grace after he finished work.

"Congratulations John," I ventured one day before the wedding "I didn't realise you were thinking of tying the knot."

"Ay, well, noobody would ever have me," he grinned sheepishly, "But Gracie's a good woman and we'll get along fine."

"Anyways," he added confidingly, "don't say nuthin, but she told me wun night that she had this dream of getting married and having the notice put in the paper. One in the eye for her family I reckon! Well I had been thinking about it, so I asked her there an' then, to marry me. I were a bit surprised when she agreed - I'm a good bit older than her ya know. So the wedding's at Holy Trinity on 11th June - no point waiting! I've got the newspaper all sorted to report it, and Gracie's as happy as can be - I've never seen her smile so much, and she's even cut down on the old beer!" he laughed contentedly.

I'd never seen John smile so much either! I wished them both well. Maybe Grace would be able to keep out of trouble now!

I didn't get to see the wedding though I saw the copy of the marriage certificate where both of them made their mark. But then I read the Berwick Journal of 13th June 1862:

"   MARRIAGE IN HIGH LIFE

On Wednesday morning, long before the statutory hour for joining in Hymen's bands the loving hearts desirous of being made one, the denizens of Church Street and the fashionable purlieus of "Shaws Lane" and Walkergate Lane were all astir, and testifying by their joyous shouts that some great event was about to occur……. And as eight o'clock struck, it became known that the cause of the festivities was the marriage of John White, bachelor, to Grace Guthrie, spinster, both of whom are well known in Berwick, and both of whom move in the very highest society! The marriage was celebrated in the parish church, and we believe the curate (unlike in some fashionable marriages, where one or two ministers have to assist the officiating clergyman) was perfectly able to perform the whole ceremony himself! After the marriage the happy pair proceeded by different routes, to their domicile, the fair bride receiving quite an ovation from admiring crowds who had turned out to welcome her home. A splendidly served 'dejeuner a la fourchette' was then partaken of, but the bridal party did NOT afterwards leave town by the express train for the continent."

No doubt the smart-alec reporter thought he was being funny, but really it was just unkind. Fortunately, neither John nor Grace could read so I hoped that no-one had told them that the reporter had made fun of them.

Whenever I saw Grace over the next few years she seemed happy and usually sober. John was looking out for her and getting her safely home at night. But then in 1865 John died. Grieving and alone, Grace now had no means of support, and being unable to pay the rent, she was soon back out on the streets. She resorted to her old comfort - the public houses, and I'm sorry to say, I often saw her much the worse for drink. It was no surprise that in 1869 she was once again in the courts (name Grace White now of course) for drunkenness. Somehow, she got off with a warning as long as she promised to take herself to the workhouse, which she did - I made sure of it!

For the rest of her life, poor Grace carried on offending, and as far as I know, when she died in 1876, she was all alone. There had never been any reconciliation with her family. I was sad to hear it. I came across many drunks during my years as a constable, but Grace Guthrie/White is the one I will never forget.

DOWNFALL OF THE NIGHTWALKERS

by Angela Winson

A mantle of snow had fallen over Berwick-upon-Tweed that day in February 1877, and as night drew in, it was a time to be in front of a crackling fire, closing the door to the cold world outside and the blackening slush now covering the pavements. A time for quiet reflection on the day's happenings but it was not to be, as outside the noise and commotion in the darkened street was deafening. Voices rose to screaming pitch as words were flung hysterically between a group of women on one side of Eastern Lane and two women of the night, each hanging on the arm of a sailor, on the other. A third sailor watched the High Street, ready to raise the alarm of any approaching police officers.

"We don't want the likes of you around here", a woman yelled, "you should be ashamed of yourself, get away to the other end of town and leave us decent folk be."

Shouts of agreement resounded along the narrow lane as two rotten apples landed at the feet of May Johnson. Infuriated she bent down to pick one up with the intention of throwing it back at the crowd but a hand on her arm stilled her.

"No May, it ain't worth it, they're just a bunch of bigots, scared they can't keep their man."

Mary Ann Murray flicked her thumb off blackened front teeth in the direction of the baying women, "I can teach you a few tricks on how to keep yer man happy if yer like," she threw back her head and cackled as she raised her skirt to reveal scruffy red bloomers.

Her action enraged the crowd even more and further abuse was hurled her way, prompting Mary Ann to raise her skirt even higher. Provocatively she swayed her hips towards her sailor friend. Unperturbed by the audience on the other side of the lane he pulled Mary Ann to him grinding his hips into hers.

May joined in the street show by unbuttoning her blouse and pushing it off her shoulder. "Men can't resist a bit of teasing from a hot-blooded woman." She ran her hands through her long black curly hair, ruffling it into disarray. "That's how yer man likes it – nice and rough!" May was grabbed by her sailor and he nuzzled her neck as his roughened hand strayed into the unbuttoned blouse. Groaning with passion, she stared straight into the eyes of a mousy woman in the crowd. "Ooh, yeah, yer want to try it hen, spice up your evenings. Yer might find yer enjoy it!"

The woman stood transfixed, one hand crept up to her neck where the top button of her blouse was securely fastened, and her other hand went to the knot of hair in the nape of her head. She blinked back unshed tears and scurried back to her front door, locking it when she had reached the safety of her home.

"That's right run away. Send your man out and I'll warm him up for yer", May called after her.

"Leave her alone May", said Mary Ann "have yer seen her man, he ain't worth going after." She turned to the now dispersing women, "None o' yer men are worth it after yer've beaten them into submission, the poor devils."

Laughing the two women returned their attention to the men they had in the palm of their hands and the rewards they would reap at the end of the night. A woman appeared with a bucket of slops and threw the contents at the shameless couples, which they neatly dodged. "You're disgusting!" she yelled as she scuttled away.

Suddenly the third sailor ran down the lane shouting a warning. The other two men untangled themselves from the women and all three set off down the steep, slippery lane towards Bridge Street and the quayside.

May and Mary Ann yelled for them to come back as they had a living to earn but it was to no avail, they were gone, swallowed up in the gloom of the cold starless night.

The last of the angered women threw final insults before retreating to the stale warmth of their homes. During the female fracas their husbands had stayed safely indoors knowing the situation could turn on them before the night was out if they got involved.

On the now empty lane the two women straightened their clothes and shivered against the cold night air. The adrenaline of a good argument and the prospect of a few shillings in their pockets had cooled. They pulled their shawls tightly across their shoulders, stamping and kicking a nearby wall to loosen the clinging wet slush off their boots, cursing their misfortune.

"What now?" asked May.

"I suppose we could try our luck in the Berwick Arms or the Brown Bear." Mary Ann grinned knowingly at her friend. "At least we'll be warm."

"Hold on", May tapped Mary Ann on the shoulder, "I think opportunity has just arrived."

Two men had turned into Eastern Lane from the High Street. Both were tall in stature, handsomely turned out in winter coats and mufflers to stave off the cold. One wore a hat and as they neared the women, he tipped it in acknowledgement.

May giggled and sauntered seductively over to him. "Hello darlin', are yer looking for a good time, well, it's yer lucky day 'cause yer just found it." She lifted his hat, put it firmly on her head and draped her arms around the man's neck, "What yer say?"

Mary Ann had honed in on the other man, "And we're cheap at half the price", she purred, "anything yer fancy in particular?" Linking her arm with his she began propelling him down Eastern Lane towards the River Tweed.

"No, my girl, you're coming with me", he said as he turned her round and pushed her in the direction of the High Street. Likewise, the man May had attached herself to untangled her arms from around his neck and lead her to the High Street.

"'Ere, watch it, what's going on?" Where yer takin' us?" the girls wailed in unison.

"Thank you, gentlemen." A deep voice filled the night air and a uniformed man stepped forward, "We'll take the ladies from here." He indicated to two other policemen who took hold of a woman each.

"You're welcome to them, Constable", said the man as he retrieved his hat, "They're not exactly our type". With an inclination of his head he bade the officer 'good night', then the two gentlemen quickly disappeared into the darkness of the night.

May and Mary Ann were furious, "Yer don't know what yer missing!"

"Yer could've had a good time!"

"We'll remember yer."

"We'll get our own back!" Their screams echoed up and down the High Street. "Yer won't get away wi' this!"

The two policemen struggled to hold the women until slowly they quietened and stood dejected, their heads bowed. May and Mary Ann shrugged off the policemen's hold on their arms and said they would walk by themselves.

"All right then," said the constable, "but it's jail for you two and then you'll be up before the Mayor and we'll see what he has to say."

On February 5th 1877 May Johnston and Mary Ann Murray, both single women, were summoned to the Town Hall. Andrew Thompson, Mayor of Berwick-upon-Tweed, presided in the courtroom and in the presence of James Purves, a respected man of the town, their crimes were read out. They each received a sentence of 14 days in prison for being *'nightwalkers and loitering and importuning passengers for the purpose of prostitution in Eastern Lane in the 3rd inst. To the annoyance of passengers and residents.'*

The women protested but to no avail. They had been in this same situation on numerous occasions and fines been issued – which they hadn't paid. They were escorted to the prison in Wallace Green that had replaced the over-crowded prison in the Town Hall, where Elizabeth Fry, the prison reformist, had visited and criticised in no uncertain terms in 1819. A scathing report from the Government was received in 1838 and finally the Town Hall prison was rendered obsolete in 1849 in favour of Wallace Green.

On Monday February 19th, May and Mary Ann stepped out into the street dishevelled and stinking from 14 days without washing properly and their uncombed hair matted into tangles. Slowly, they trudged down Walkergate towards the High Street.

"I suppose our rooms have been taken now and I need a bath. Got any money stashed?" asked Mary Ann, pulling her shawl over her head.

May laughed. "Oh yeah, made of money me. Why do yer think I was out with yer that night? I was skint. Well, at least we've had a roof over our heads for a couple of weeks but what do we do now? Where do we go?"

"Maybe we could go to Newcastle. Better pickings, more money," Mary Ann strode quickly down the High Street as snow began to fall, "but first we'd have to earn some money for a train ticket to get us there."

"Aye, maybe," agreed May, running to catch up with her, "and this time we'll be more careful who we hook up with."

Walking arm in arm they mulled over the idea of going to Newcastle but finally agreed Berwick-upon-Tweed was more favourable with the passing ships full of hungry sailors who had plenty of money burning holes in their pockets.

Laughing they quickened their pace as they approached the Berwick Arms. Nodding to each other in a silent agreement they pushed open the door moseyed in. "Hello boys, we're back." May's cackling voice rose above the hubbub of the crowded bar, "Who's getting the beers in then? It's been a long, dry fourteen days."

From behind the closed doors a muffled cheer broke the evenings silence. Large snowflakes began to envelop the streets of Berwick and the imposing Town Hall, where sentences of jail, transportation and hangings were harshly imposed. Over the years many lives were lost or radically changed forever – with the exception of the two nightwalkers of course.

The gallery on the prison hulk Warrior

WHAT HAPPENED TO JAMES COOK?

by Angela Winson

It was a cold January night 1877 when James Cook staggered out of the White Swan Inn in Castlegate, with the help of an irate landlord.

"Get out and stay out!" he yelled, punctuating the order with a kick to the unfortunate man's backside.

"Just one more drink." The words were slurred as James leaned against the wall for support. "One more little drink for the road. I've got money." He delved into the depths of his trouser pocket and produced a handful of coins, along with a ragged handkerchief which fell onto the pavement. Bending to retrieve it he toppled, sniggering in the inane manner only a drunk can. Two gentlemen came through the door and made to move round him. In one quick move James grabbed the coat hem of the nearest one. "Just one for the road."

"Get away with you!" the man snapped, tugging his coat out of James's hands.

"Tell him to serve me with a drink then." Waving a hand in the direction of the red-faced landlord he continued to protest. "Tell him I can pay. Look!" He opened his hand and his money fell to the ground next to his handkerchief. "Aw, look what you've made me do." Grabbing the man's coat again James hauled himself up and pushed his angered face close to the now startled man. "Pick it up", he spluttered. "Go on, pick it up!" He dragged his sleeve across his saliva laden mouth as he tried to maintain his menacing stance but his knees slowly sagged until he was once again on his hands and knees.

The two men sidestepped the pathetic sight. "Come Jonathan, leave this disgusting ragbag to the task of retrieving his own money." Bidding the landlord good night, they made their way homeward.

"All I want is a drink", he whimpered as he picked up his pennies one by one.

"Well, you won't get it here", retorted the now shivering landlord. "Away with you." He went inside and firmly shut the door against the cold of the night and James Cook.

The dull streetlight cast an eerie shadow on the wall, portraying a sad broken man. He blew his nose into the already filthy handkerchief and stuffed it into his pocket. Having picked up his coins James staggered up, gasping with exertion. His breath spiralled white against the darkness. "I need a drink", he mumbled, then squaring his shoulders he yelled defiantly at the closed door. "I don't need to frequent the White Swan Inn, and neither do you!" His last words were flung in the direction of a man and woman walking on the other side of the road. He took off his hat and executed a sweeping bow, nearly toppling to the pavement again. Laughing loudly, he straightened up and continued his rant. "My money ain't good enough in there, not shiny enough, it was last night and the night afore that but tonight?" he sliced the air with his hand, "no, not shiny enough. But…" he lurched into the middle of the road, "but… the landlord at the Red Lion'll take it, you mark my words, shiny or no." The couple hurried on ignoring the antics of the highly inebriated James as he continued his journey singing bawdy songs at the top of his voice.

He pulled up his collar as he passed under Scotsgate, the crisp January air began to parch his throat as he sang and passers-by dodged his flailing arms as he tried to grab the ladies. "Dance with me", he hollered as he swayed to his tunes. Their disgusted response only made him laugh and spin giddily until he stopped and stared at a familiar face. "I know you", he stated solemnly "come, join me in a drink at the Red Lion." Not getting a reply he shrugged his shoulders. "Ain't I good enough to drink with? Well, it's your loss." James stumbled on, still singing, not realising he'd been talking to his own reflection in the shop window of Skelly the butcher. From an upper window a voice urged him to 'shut that racket' which of course James ignored and sang even more loudly and bawdy.

Finally, he arrived at the Red Lion. Slapping his money onto the bar he demanded a pint of the finest ale, "And make it quick", he said, "I have a raging thirst awaiting to be quenched."

Suddenly there was a commotion by the door and the smoke-filled room fell silent. A couple of men sidled out of the back door as James thumped the bar demanding to be served.

The policeman who had stilled the atmosphere went over to James and laid a hand on his shoulder. "Come on lad, time to go home." James swung round shrugging off the hand. "Leave me be!", he yelled, "I just want a pint!"

The policeman stumbled and fell against a table sending glasses of beer crashing to the floor. Quickly regaining his balance, he grabbed James's arm pushing it up his back as he propelled him towards the door. "James Cook, I'm arresting you for being drunk and disorderly." Once outside a second policeman helped to escort the protesting James to Wallace Green jail and there to await being called before the court.

Present in the Town Hall on the morning of January 20th 1877 was Andrew Thompson Esq. – Mayor of Berwick upon Tweed and A R Lowry as James Cook stood alone before them. The only words he uttered was to confirm his name and that he was a resident of Berwick. He exhibited no response when charged with being drunk and disorderly. Subsequently, he was put on remand until noon the following Thursday.

In the confinement of the jail his behaviour fluctuated between violence and depression, possibly as a result of alcohol deprivation. Over the ensuing days he began to act in such an imbalanced manner that a doctor was summoned to 'attend and give an opinion of the prisoner's state of mind'.

On January 25th, in the Justice Rooms, Andrew Thompson Esq. - Mayor of Berwick upon Tweed, Alex R Lowry and Rob C Fluker were awaiting the arrival of James Cook. Shortly they were to learn that the offender had been certified as 'too ill to appear'. In his absence he was remanded to the next petty sessions.

During the next seven days James Cook's health did not improve. In the Justice Room on February 1st and officiated by Mayor Andrew Thompson, A R Lowry, Rob Thompson, Rob C Fluker, Jas Purves and D Loyon passed sentence. James Cook – 'remanded to this day on charge of being drunk and disorderly' – was discharged as 'no evidence was offered'.

However, a Medical Certificate was produced claiming that although the defendant was well in body, he was deemed to be not of sound mind.

The police were instructed to deliver him to the Workhouse Infirmary – St George's County Asylum in Morpeth, to be detained in trial.

The puzzling thing is there are no records of James Cook ever arriving there. Was he taken to an Asylum in an alternative county? Did he elude the officers during his transit? If he did, perhaps he changed his name and fled the country, who knows; but either way James Cook, labourer of Berwick upon Tweed, disappeared into the mists of time.

John Tait 1883

Poaching - was it worth it?
by Stella McLaren

The silence was broken by the snap of the twig I had inadvertently stepped on. Glancing cautiously around, I waited, frozen to the spot, listening for any disturbance. The minutes seemed to crawl by. Thankfully for me, nothing was stirring. It wouldn't do to be caught red handed again.

My name is John Tait, I used to be a labourer, working in and around the town of Berwick-upon-Tweed. A lovely place with the sea as the boundary on one side and the land surrounding the rest. Berwick was nestled in the middle, safe within the Elizabethan walls.

I ask you. What was a poor man to do? Work was hard to come by. Honest work that is. Plenty of illicit goings on, if you knew where to look, but you had to watch your back. There were plenty around who would be only too happy to whisper your name to the police.

I had a shack deep in the woods where I kept the tools of my trade, far away from prying eyes. For obvious reasons, and the nature of my profession, deliveries had to be transacted under cover of darkness.

I continued cautiously on into the wood, checking my snares for rabbits. I made a few coppers, selling them to the local hostelries, round by the back door of course. My favourite haunt was the Hen and Chicken's, where I could usually persuade Elsie to give me a bowl of steaming hot stew or broth and if I was very lucky a pint of ale to wash it all down. I made enough for my modest needs, and along with my foraging skills, which some unenlightened people would term poaching, I survived.

On January 22nd 1882 I had the misfortune of being caught by PC. Young. I'd had 5 rabbits hanging from my belt along with my snares. Being brought before the court I was ordered to pay a fine of 10 shillings. Where was I to get that sort of money? I managed to escape and fled back to the woods. Then on the 12th of September misfortune struck again. Thank goodness it was PC. Young, for with a twist of my body, I managed to break free and ran off, giving him the slip. It would have been a very different story with the squire's game keeper. He and I had run ins before. A stranger to the truth when it suited him. A right concocted story he would have told the squire I'll be bound, and him not noted for leniency.

Still, not a bad night's work if I do say so, 5 plump rabbits should fetch a couple of shillings. Making my way stealthily out of the woods, I glanced up at the sky. Plenty of cloud cover, was it worth risking a trip to the Hen and Chickens? Or should I wait for tonight? Maybe if I took the risk now Elsie could be cajoled into giving me some breakfast. A nice thick slice of ham and eggs, it was enough to get the juices flowing. That settled it, the Hen and Chickens it would be.

I set off down the lane, as quiet as I could and keeping well into the tree line. I might well need a quick escape if I heard anything suspicious. I'd had a good run since evading capture last year, it wouldn't do to drop my guard now. It was a tidy hike to Berwick through the fields, fortunately mostly downhill.

What happened next was my own silly fault. I couldn't have been paying proper attention, for as I neared my goal, a voice came out of the gloom.

"Got you my lad," said the voice I knew.

"I've been keeping a regular lookout on these paths to the pubs, knowing if I was patient I would eventually catch you."

My luck had finally run out, no chance of escaping this time. It was PC Dickson who had grabbed my collar that night and marched me off gleefully to the new gaol in the Town Hall. Up the stairs, the rabbits and snares banging against my legs. This made it difficult for me to climb safely, which I am sure was his intention. Poking me from behind and generally giving me verbal abuse we went up and up. At the top there were different levels of security, where was he going to put me?

"In you go." PC Dickson said pushing me into a room.

"I'll take the rabbits now, and those". Pointing to the snares.

Slumping down on the cold floor, I knew I was going to cop it now. As if to add insult to injury, I could hear PC Dickson whistling as he went back down the stairs, to share out my ill-gotten gains with his collegues. Life was so unfair.

I spent the rest of the night worrying about what my fate might be. Poachers were not popular. Punishments such as flogging, branding, imprisonment and fines, were commonplace. I didn't fancy any of them.

All too soon morning came, the light gradually penetrating the cell. I must have dozed off at some point for the next sound I heard was the key turning in the lock.

"Right, let's be having you, it doesn't do to keep the court waiting."

PC Dickson stood in the doorway a bunch of keys hanging from his finger.

When we entered the court room, I looked up and saw to my horror that W Orde Esq and Reverend Canon Baldwin were presiding over the court that day. These two had extensive lands between them and had no time for the excuses of poachers. Just my luck, I don't think, my heart sank.

"John Tait you are charged that on the 12th of October, in this year of our Lord 1883, you were arrested for being in possession of 5 rabbits, having been unlawfully captured on private property. How do you plead."

"Guilty, sir." I mumbled, knowing fine well I could do nothing else.

"Have you nothing to say for yourself." Canon Baldwin demanded.

"Sir, I'm a labourer, and there's no work to be had at the daily hiring. What work there is, goes to the younger men."

"That's no excuse for taking what doesn't belong to you." he continued.

A brief whispered conversation took place between the two men. W Orde Esq then spoke.

"John Tait you are found guilty and are hereby ordered to pay a 10-shilling fine. Furthermore, it is noted that you have similar charges outstanding. These will each incur a 10-shilling fine. Can you pay."

"Sirs", I stammered, "There is no way I can pay a fine of such magnitude."

"John Tait, you are hereby sentenced to 14 days imprisonment with hard labour, for each offence. Take him away."

As I was led away, my heart was pounding, PC Dickson whispered spitefully in my ear.

"Hard labour, that is exactly that, and it will be so hard for you. Think you can make a fool of the law; well you will soon find out differently." One sentence was bad enough to contemplate. All my offences had been added together, complete with the added misery of the threats which I knew would be carried out.

As they say, "be sure your sins will find you out".

I don't know whether I will survive.

I had a little drink or Two

by Stella McLaren

Berwick Petty Sessions 26th January 1886 before A Robertson, Esq and L.T. Fleming Esq. Court now in Session. Bring in the first defendant.

Hello, my name is Fanny McCarthy. I'm single and live in the town of Berwick-upon-Tweed. I don't suppose you'll have heard of me; my sort ain't famous. Still I have a story to tell just like anyone else.

I live in Walkergate Lane. It's nothing to write home about, but its where I live. I make ends meet by doing a bit of cleaning, scrubbing and the like up at the big house on the Elizabethan walls. With what I earn and leftovers from the kitchen that cook very kindly gives me I make do. Life is hard for us ordinary folk; work is hard to come by for the men especially. Us women do what we can but the wages women earn is lower than for the men. Life just isn't fair.

I like a sing song and a drink on a weekend, I earn my drink by singing in the pubs. I've got a nice voice if I say so and I like to sing songs popular in the music halls. As the men get tipsy, the more generous they become and I have many a drink lined up on the old piano. I's always had a bit of trouble with the mother's ruin, an it's all too easy to have one too many then the songs become quite bawdy and loud. The locals don't seem to mind though and egg me on. Some of the more toffee-nosed locals don't like it and complain to the local police. Honestly, they can't let a body have a bit of fun. I can always do with an extra shilling or two, and for a little extra activity if you get my meaning, there's easy pickings on the weekend. You don't have too many mates in my game so we stay to our own patch mostly, no need to be courting trouble. We's fortunate as there's no shortage of soldiers around, with the barracks just up the road on Ravensdowne.

It was January 1886, the children in the big house had just received their copy of the book by the newly acclaimed author Robert Louis Stephenson. His book titled Kidnapped was a late Christmas present from their father. You might well be surprised that I had heard of a book let alone know the title. I's used to like to sneak up the back stairs to the nursery and sit outside the door while the children were read a chapter before bedtime. Fancy somebody writing about such goings on a body could hardly believe it were possible.

Well you know a little about me now so I'll fill you in on some of the more disreputable parts of my life that led to me being in my present predicament.

I's really don't know how it happened, that gradual fall from grace to gutter where unfortunately you now find me. I lost my job at the big house and the perks that went with it, and sadly I'll never hear the end of the story seems

I's wasn't the sort they wanted around, a bad influence they called it. I blame it on the demon drink, it seems that when you's get a taste for it, you need more and more to satisfy you. Singing in the pubs didn't bring enough drink to satisfy my cravings and so what used to be a little side line where I was more discerning in my choice of companions became well, I'm ashamed to say, anyone who had a shilling or two for a quickie up the back lane. I had been caught some times before, but mostly the police gave me a warning and moved me on.

This evening saw me hit bottom, earlier in the evening I had been caught in Walkergate Lane with four soldiers but I must still have been reasonably sober enough not to cause a disturbance. Later that night I was in a yard at the top of Ravensdowne, when another woman came to my patch as I saw it. This of course led to an altercation which got loud and involved some punching, hair pulling and ended up with us both on the ground, each trying to get the upper hand. PC Moor was out on his patrol when he came upon us. After hauling us off each other he started to berated us for disturbing the peace. We were told to move along and go home to sleep it off. I have no idea what got into me but I saw red and well the language I used was choice, I cursed him, his mother and anyone else I could think of, swearing and calling him every foul name I knew. I was unceremoniously marched off to the gaol to spend the night in the cells before appearing in court the next morning.

This morning brought me before the honourable gentlemen of the bench. It shook me to hear all the nasty things that were said about me. Drunk and disorderly, fighting, soliciting etc etc. Four other convictions were brought up and PC Moor told of the numerous warnings I had received as well.

It didn't take the gentlemen long to deliberate on their verdict. I was described as an incorrigible character and sentenced to 14 days imprisonment. Help! I was shaking now and it wasn't just from the withdrawal of the drunken haze I was habitually in. You might think the sentence was lenient but for me it might have been for life. No drink, so going cold turkey would give me withdrawal symptoms and accompanied by the hard work and yes it was hard washing sheets in the laundry in the heat and steam and long back breaking hours sapping your strength. It made you prey to abuse from fellow inmates who liked to pick on the weaker and more vulnerable women. It was going to be a living hell.

I made myself a vow if I survived, I would never touch a drop ever again.

(Till the next time.)

The Journalist
by Alan Dumble

It was in the days long before Google and the internet. For my sins I was employed by a well-known Northern newspaper, as a trainee journalist otherwise known as 'Hey you, get the coffees', the general dogsbody of the office. To my surprise one day my boss came across and said, "Get yourself up to Berwick and come back with an article about 'Salmon Fishing on the Tweed." 'The season has just started so we will also need a selection of appropriate photographs. Reasonable expenses will be paid,I emphasise 'reasonable' we are not the Daily Telegraph you know."

I was delighted. I could see it now. Not the front page but a full page, featured article with my photograph centre page. 'Oh bliss'. As the train pulled into a grubby station, I glanced around at my surroundings, 'Oh bliss' did not now seem the appropriate phrase. Still with my briefcase in hand, notebook ready in my pocket I took a taxi into town, a three-minute ride. After being dropped off at my hotel, shown to my room etc., I decided to take a walk around. I began to feel rather depressed the more I explored the town. It gave out the feeling that amidst the general gloom there was somehow a glorious walled town just waiting with its wealth of fascinating architecture to be discovered and take its place as one of Europe's leading heritage towns.

By chance I came across the town's library so took the opportunity to do some research. The most helpful librarian set before me a generous quantity of archived papers and gave me an excellent resume of the 'Salmon Industry'. I then started flicking through the documents and was delighted to find the reduced photocopy of a poster from the late 1880s. It proclaimed '£5 Reward for information leading to the apprehension of the person or persons who maliciously cut salmon nets hanging at the Sandstell fishery, Sandstell Road.'

That evening I decided to have a wander in the area it referred to and, having read quite a few Agatha Christie novels, dropped into one of the local pubs to see if I could pick up any gossip or information about the Salmon Industry. Frankly I was a bit worried about some of the characters around me talking amongst themselves glancing across at me with not exactly friendly stares. However, as the evening drew on, more pints (on expenses) downed, I gradually became involved in their conversations and their curiosity as to what brought me to Berwick. I didn't give too much away and nor did they, although I did get to know a lot about how things have changed from the old days. How once there were 55 or so shiels (or batts) rather like shepherds huts alongside the river but they rapidly dwindled until there was only one functioning, and how there used to be great rivalry amongst the different fishing groups which occasionally turned violent. They changed the subject at this point unwilling to discuss this further and moved on to the subject of poaching. If I really needed to know about this then I would have to meet the son of the 'Border Rover'. The Rover, I was told being a tall fierce looking solitary man with an unkempt black beard, bloodshot eyes shaggy eyebrows and never without his battered felt hat. By this time I sensed they weren't too happy about my inquisitiveness so I did not bring out my copy of the poster but changed the subject to Berwick Rangers.

As I left the pub at closing time one of the more friendly of the group, who worked for a local printing firm muttered to me on passing,

"Take care on the way back, your questions were a bit too near the knuckle for two of the remaining coble men."

The following day was spent primarily taking photographs of salmon related buildings, and a few fishermen at work, plus meeting some of the Berwick Advertiser staff who were most helpful with my quest. Again, I was warned that beneath the surface, ever since the date of my poster, two families have been at loggerheads; enmity passing from father to son and that it took very little to spark off severe violence because of the feud between the families.

Just as I neared the pub that evening I was accosted by two, what in these circumstances, seem to be normally described as 'heavies'. Thrust against the wall and a warning gentle bash of my head against the bricks, they then spoke.

"We hear that you have been quizzing our mates about a certain copy of a poster. Well, you interfering little sod, we are going to take you to the original."

I was blindfolded and manhandled into their car. It was driven for what seemed several miles without a word being said. I was heaved out of the car and dragged along a pathway by them holding my feet and with my head banging on the paving. Through a door up some stairs and into what, when my blindfold was removed, I saw was a sparsely furnished room.

"Right sunshine, feast your eyes on that. You didn't know we painted houses did you?" My heart sank. In the criminal world' to paint a house' is to kill a man - this much I knew. The painting referred to the blood of the victim or victims splattering the walls as in the infamous killings carried out by Charles Manson and his followers. Then, to my amazement there, on the blood splattered wall, was a framed enlargement of the poster and underneath it in capital letters was written; possibly in blood, 'Yes we know who did it, but he will never do it again!"

I was left speechless. Much to my relief I was then blindfolded and dragged off to the car. Reaching our destination, I was unceremoniously pulled out of the car and given another 'going over'. The car left just as I lost consciousness. Later on, the following day I 'came-to' finding myself lying in a most comfortable hospital bed aching all over. A cheerful nurse came across, "Hello dear, well luckily no bones broken but plenty beautiful bruises. We thought at first here's another Saturday night drunk - but with no alcohol signs and sights of blood you must have greatly offended a few people. At least they dumped you near to the A and E department," and with a wide grin, "We are sure you are going to survive but I should keep well away from the sort of company you were with last night as no doubt you will. I assume they weren't friends of yours."

"No way" I said with difficulty. "By the way," she continued "a rather irate and desperate gentleman was on the telephone asking whether a person answering to your description was by any chance in our care and if there was I was to tell him and I quote 'Get off your bloody backside and return immediately, papers don't run without stories you know.'"

I reluctantly left Berwick A and E and eventually found myself no longer the investigative journalist of my imagination but left to report on W.I., local football matches etc. A story on 'Salmon fishing on the Tweed' did appear, not mine, but one by a guest writer from the Berwick Advertiser. Nevertheless, I kid myself that one day

I might even find the courage to return to Berwick and find out whether indeed my assailants knew 'who done it' or whether, as the saying goes, 'discretion is the better part of valour!' Yes, you guess correctly, 'discretion' won and I am now working as a very 'civil' civil servant. Incidently, when I had arrived home after my adventure, what did my mother quite innocently say to me following a welcoming chat?

"Darling I think daddy is going to have the house painted.

My knees buckled!

Whose Horse are You?

by Homer Lindsay

I found myself in trouble at the 1891 Easter Quarter Sessions for the Borough of Berwick over the purchase of a horse. I had bought a brown mare at auction in Wooler on 15th December from George Cockburn for £4.5s. who agreed to deliver it to me in Spittal. When he failed to deliver, I kept asking for the horse, but Cockburn always put me off. On 13th January I went to their stables, took my horse and led it away having told him beforehand what I was going to do.

It is now 3rd April and I am in the dock. The Recorder, W T Greenhow sits on the bench with the Mayor and some others I do not know. The jury is on my right. My counsel, Mr Blake, is to the left of me. He gives me a smile of reassurance; I feel far from reassured. I've been told that witnesses will be examined and cross-examined by Counsel, but I will not be allowed to speak. Mr Blake will do so in my defence.

I am frightened.

An official stands up, "David Scott, you are charged with having feloniously stolen and led away a brown mare, value £5, the property of Alexander Cockburn of Berwick. How do you plead?"

"Not Guilty," I reply.

Mr Hamilton, the prosecutor, outlines to the jury the case against me, then calls Alexander Cockburn to the witness stand. That's George's brother. They are both horse dealers. He tells of New Year's Day when he, his other brother, William, and I were coming back from a trip to Weetwood. He is saying I asked William to exchange my brown mare for one of his.

"We were in the Sanderson's public house in Lowick," Alexander is saying, "and we met a man, Thomas Smith. He was interested in our horses. One of those was the horse which had been exchanged for the mare. Smith looked at this horse and asked whose it was. The defendant replied that it was his and asked Smith to buy it."

"Scott asked £15 for it but the animal was half-bred," says Alexander, "Smith agreed to pay £3.10s. He paid that to Scott and I saw Smith take away the horse."

No! William was paid £3.10s, and he gave me 4s as commission. I want to shout out that this man is untruthful, but Mr Blake had warned me to keep quiet.

Alexander is now saying that on the next day he bought my brown mare from his brother George for £4.

Mr Blake rises to cross-examine. He is asking Alexander if he is an honest man.

"I have led an honest life these last six years."

"When were you last convicted of larceny?"

"It was a long time ago," says Cockburn.

"Was it in 1889, two years ago?" asks Mr Blake.

"Perhaps."

"Larceny from the person; a month's hard labour?"

"Yes," admits Alexander Cockburn.

"Another man was charged with you. What was his name?"

"William Grant."

"Was he with you in Wooler?"

"No, that was someone else."

"Was William Grant the man in whose name the horse was put into the sale ring at Wooler?"

"I believe so, but I had nothing to do with that."

"Which horse do you speak of now?" interrupts the Recorder, "It is difficult to keep track of all these horses."

"William Cockburn's horse, your Honour, sold for £3.10s at Lowick to Thomas Smith," replies Mr Blake.

"Were you present at the auction sale at Wooler when this horse was sold?"

"My brother told me it did not sell."

"You say you bought the brown mare from your brother, George. When did you pay him for it and how much?"

"I paid George £4 for it on the day after New Year's Day."

"He did not tell you that the defendant was going to take the horse if it was not delivered to him?"

"No" says Alexander.

William Cockburn is now being called to give evidence. He is also a horse dealer. William gives corroborating evidence and confirms he was present when I gave money to George.

Mr Blake rises, "Mr Cockburn, you say you exchanged your horse for the brown mare owned by David Scott. This horse, where did you get it from?"

"Eh, I got it from a gentleman."

"What is this gentleman's name?"

"That is my business. It is common to get a horse as a present. It was a gentleman who gave me this horse. The horse is my property.

"Was this the horse that was put in the ring in the name of Grant?"

"Yes."

"Did Grant give you the horse?"

"No."

"Explain why the horse was put into the sale ring under Grant's name."

"He said to do so. It might sell better in his name than mine."

"I have no doubt of that," laughed Mr Blake.

The jury are laughing too!

"You thought you would get a better sale in Grant's name than your own?"

"Yes, because he is not a dealer."

"Was Grant there with you?"

"Yes."

"What is he?"

"He is a tailor to trade."

"You thought it was a good idea to put a horse into the sale ring in the name of a tailor?"

The Recorder says, "Tailors are not known for their knowledge of horses."

There is more laughter!

Mr Blake continues, "Did you not say before in the Magistrates court where this case was first brought that Scott had asked for delivery of the mare, but your brother refused until Scott paid the balance of the purchase money?"

"I did not hear him ask for delivery of the mare. If I said that before the Magistrates, it is a mistake. He said the mare could stay, and he would pay for her keep. Scott did not tell me in the Cock and Lion public house that he was going to settle with my brother George."

"Did he not say he would pay the 15s due on the purchase of the horse?"

"No, I never heard him."

"Scott acted as your agent in the sale to Thomas Smith, didn't he?"

"No."

"Did you not give him 4s?"

"Not a farthing. Nor did my brother."

"Are you an honest witness?"

"I am a reformed, honest man."

"You were last convicted in 1885, of robbery with violence at the Assizes and were sentenced to 20 months. You were also convicted in 1880 of stealing a silver watch, sentenced to 18 months. You are well known at the Police Court. In fact, have you not been some 21 or 22 times in a court of law?"

Mr Hamilton rises and says, "You have a longer experience of law than my learned friend."

Everyone in the court is laughing, except me.

"Since 1885, have you ever been charged with any dishonesty at all?" asks the Prosecutor.

"Never."

My Counsel has made a good job of exposing the dishonesty of these two witnesses. George Cockburn is now called to the witness stand. Mr Hamilton is asking him the same questions but nothing new is revealed.

Mr Blake asks him, "Do you know a man named Grant?"

"Yes," replies George.

"What is he?"

"A labourer."

Alexander said he was a tailor!

"What did he get for lending his name to the sale of the horse at Wooler?"

"Half a crown."

"Did you know the gentleman who gave the horse to your brother William?"

"No."

Mr Blake asks, "Do you have an uncle called Alexander Cockburn, living in Coldstream?"

"Yes."

"Were you in the Cock and Lion on 15th December?"

"Yes. We went there after the auction."

"Call William Simpson to the stand."

He is a carter from Tweedmouth. He is saying he was at the Cock and Lion public house on 15th December and heard George Cockburn ask the prisoner for 15s and 15s for the keep of the mare.

"Scott said he would pay the former but not the latter," he says.

Thomas Smith comes to the witness stand. He is a carter from Lowick.

Mr Hamilton asks him, "Did you buy a horse from the defendant?"

"Yes. For £3.10s. It was not a bad one to look at."

"But a bad one to move," interrupts the Recorder.

The crowd laughs again. I am not finding much to laugh about! He is saying that I represented the horse as a good one.

"What was wrong with it?"

"Everything."

"Were the Cockburn's there?"

"Yes. William Cockburn said he would have bought the horse if it had not been for fear of his aunt."

Everyone is laughing now!

"Useless creature," says Mr Blake.

Mr Hamilton says, "That was a joke I suppose."

"Not a joke for me. David Scott took me in. He asked £10 for the horse but came down to £3.10s. Even that was too much."

"Were the Cockburn's talking up the horse?"

"Yes. They said it was a good horse."

The Police Superintendent is called to give evidence. He confirmed that I had complained to him that Alexander Cockburn was accusing me of theft, and that Cockburn had made a complaint that I had stolen his horse.

Mr Hamilton is saying, "That concludes the case for the prosecution," and sits down.

Mr Blake says, "I do not intend to call any witnesses for the defence."

I am thunderstruck! I am sure to be convicted. I am innocent!

Mr Hamilton stands to sum up the case for the prosecution, "Although the defence have tried to blacken the characters of Alexander and William Cockburn, there were other credible witnesses to the transactions. I submit to you, the jury, that the case is proved, and you should deliver a verdict of guilty."

Mr Blake rises to make the case for the defence, "There are other courts beside this one for justice to be obtained in this case. Members of the jury, do you not think it strange that when a dispute arose between the parties the prosecutor should have chosen this court, and charged the prisoner with a criminal offence, thus preventing him giving evidence on oath about the transaction. You should know that Alexander Cockburn from Coldstream is uncle to the prosecutor and of the Cockburn brothers. The defence is that Scott simply acted as William's agent in the sale of the horse at Lowick and that he did not exchange animals at all. The prisoner denies absolutely the story of swapping horses. He took the brown mare because he believed he had a right to the horse. If the jury thinks that the man had reasonable grounds for thinking he had a right to act as he did, they should acquit him."

The Recorder is summing up the case for the jury who then leave the court to consider their verdict. I am trembling with fear. I am sure they will convict me. There is a commotion across the court. The jury are coming back in, after just a few minutes! What can this mean? I am told to stand. I am shaking!

"What is your verdict," asks the clerk.

"Not Guilty."

I am free!

"The most healthy and pleasant gaol in the Kingdom"??

by Alan Dumble

Jamie was always rather nervous when he was ordered to make the Berwick delivery. He had never forgotten his first visit. This was to meet the gentleman always referred to as 'The Boss'. He had been recommended by a pal to a character dubbed 'The Controller', who needed a replacement for a gang member who had 'messed up' a job for the The Boss; and was now ensconced on a transportation ship waiting in the Thames soon to be leaving for virtual slavery in Australia. After a brief interview and a warning that any hint of revealing details of his proposed work with The Firm would lead to either a termination of his life or a loss of various limbs, he gathered he had been accepted into The Firm.

As it was getting late he decided to stay in the Hen and Chicken Inn as travellers were allowed to stay for one evening within the town walls before moving on. He fell in with a drinking party of some soldiers billeted there and had quite an uproarious night, even making a profit in a drunken game of cards. This quite appealed to him and so the following day he thought he might extend his stay and spend another night in the town. This proved a mistake as he wasn't aware of the reason for the curfew bell which rang at 8pm, and he continued with another drunken card game. Shortly afterwards there was some shouting and swearing and he found himself confronted by the town constable wielding a hefty stick.

He was informed that non-residents were only allowed to spend one night in the town. He was given five minutes to collect his belongings. Then, he had to state which gate he wished to leave the town by. Any tardiness then, that hefty stick would be used to spur him on. Needless to say he left via the Cow Gate within minutes.

With that lesson learned he now hoped that by removing his long beard and long hair he would not be recognised by the constables on his next visits. In fact he was very pleased with his new look - most useful in attracting the young ladies, he hoped.

The cart was finally loaded with the contraband whisky, well hidden under a massive load of potatoes and other vegetables. The journey to Berwick from Tillmouth usually took three or four hours or a bit longer if he called in at the Salutation on the way. Anyhow here he was having crossed over the famous old bridge. At the checkpoint gate he dismounted, as carters were not allowed to ride on their carts inside the walls and attached his name boards to the sides of the cart, another of the regulations to be observed.

Having exchanged gossip with the inspector and paid his dues he continued along Bridge Street joining the string of carts going to the market. At the market he glanced around and caught the eye of his controller, raised his eyebrows and he in turn gave a thanks up sign. He walked across and making sure their conversation was unheard by others in the crowd, assured the gentleman that the delivery was the usual but, as he had not been paid for the last one, he insisted that he must have both last week's and this together. "Getting a bit above yourself aren't you? Making demands now. I'll see what the boss has to say but if you get on the wrong side of him I shudder to think what might happen."

Later that evening another member of the gang sided up to him muttered "Be outside the Town Hall at nine-o-clock, good luck you will be needing it". Jamie duly arrived outside the Town Hall as darkness closed in and was met by the Controller. There were a few other shady looking characters around and for some reason several ladders. "Right sonny Jim - up you go - the Boss is waiting." Jamie was unaware that the top floor of the Hall was used as the town gaol and the gentleman debtors were allowed to use an adjacent flat roof for exercise and conduct of business whilst the felons and villains were confined to their cells.

The boss strode across. "Right my lad, it's up to you - you either obey my orders or you are in big trouble." He turned around and bellowed "Constable, Constable, quick as you can, I'm being assaulted." Jamie stared in disbelief as his arms were forced behind his back. As he was marched off the boss shouted, "Two hours of 'tippy toe' should be enough."

He was dragged into one of the cells and his wrists were manacled to two iron rings hanging from the ceiling. The warders then pulled upon the chains and his arms were raised above his head until his feet cleared the floor. He was then lowered a little until his feet barely touched the floor his arms and back already feeling painful.

"Thanks lads that's fine" said the Boss giving Jamie's legs a kick. Jamie glanced around and was sure he saw money being handed over but did not dare to make a remark. It seemed the longest two hours of his life as the pain grew worse and worse. After what seemed an eternity the cell door was unlocked. "Ok" said the boss "you can remain like this until morning and then face a sentence of Transportation or you can agree never to question my decisions again".

A few years later the Boss called the Gang meeting to order. "Right men, I've decided to step back a little. From now on for all the general running of the business, Jamie here will be giving the orders". Thankfully for Jamie there appeared to be mutual approval from the gathered villains. Shades of the notorious reivers amongst his ancestors came into his mind. Surely, he thought, they would be looking down with pleasure!

A Bedtime Tale

by Alan Dumble

"Grandpop, grandpop you did promise me another story for bedtime tonight" said the little girl. "One of those you make up please not one of those in my story book."

"Did I really my darling? Well into bed you go and I'll move this armchair to beside your bed and I'll do my best to think of one."

"Yes, yes. Oh, and I promise not to go to sleep before the end."

"Do you remember the one about the little boy called 'Oliver in the workhouse?' Well this one starts in a workhouse not far away in The Greens area of Berwick.

It was there that one night the nurse on duty in charge of the baby and childrens' section heard a knocking on the workhouse door. She tried not to disturb the sleeping children and made her way down the corridor, but the knocking had now stopped. Nevertheless she opened the door. It was a dark and rainy night. She looked around but not a soul was to be seen. Just as she was about to close the door she heard a small noise. She looked down and there was a cardboard box with a note pinned to it. She brought it inside and closed the door wondering what on earth it could be. The note was written in very poor handwriting and all it said was "Please, oh please, take care of it". She opened the box and to her surprise the 'it' was a beautiful little baby girl wrapped in two very worn but very clean blankets. She carried the box along to her private room.

Removing the baby from the box she realised that the child must be only a few days old. She managed to find a feeding bottle and some milk and cradled the baby in her arms. The baby gurgled her delight and the nurse was overcome with love for her. Then not having any children of her own, she decided that 'come what may', she would adopt her and not let her be sent away to the foundlings' hospital."

"Oh thank goodness," said the grandchild, "the foundlings' hospital does not sound very nice at all and the nurse seems such a lovely person."

"Indeed she was and, because she was so well liked, she managed to convince the authorities that, with the help of her mother and father, she would be quite capable of bringing up the child and making sure when she was older that she became a regular attender at the Blue School in Ravensdowne.

Well, as years went by, the little girl was now a young lady and so loved her mother that she determined that she too would become a nurse. Luckily for her a brand new Infirmary had opened a few years earlier in Berwick near to the workhouse and was prepared to accept her for training as a nurse. She was delighted and after qualifying soon became a valued member of the staff.

As she reached retirement age and her beloved mother had died several years earlier she decided to spend her retirement in Tweedmouth in a nice little cottage next door to a young couple with a baby daughter. Not having married she found herself welcome as a convenient babysitter and emergency pram pusher. As the child grew older what fun they had playing at hospital nurses with bandages, splints and pretend medicines. The child started school and she in turn was set upon becoming a nurse. When she was fourteen 'Gran' took very ill and died gently and quietly with a smile upon her face and the child holding her hand having just promised that she too was definitely going to become a nurse".

"Oh Grandad, did she, did she? Please, please tell me yes"

"It was indeed 'yes'. She was to grow to be one of the best liked nurses and midwives in the north of England. So well had she become known for her good work that she went to Buckingham Palace to receive a big honour called the M.B.E."

"And when she was old like you what did she do?"

"Well so many good things it would take too long to tell but one thing she did was to write stories, long and short, and encouraged many people to write their own tales."

"Oh grandad you cheat! I never know whether your stories are true or not! I've guessed who the lady was. She is the lovely lady in that photograph in your study handing you a prize certificate for a story you had written. She asked me if I would sing 'All things bright and beautiful' for her then clapped her hands and said that it was one of her favourite hymns and gave me a bag of sweets. I'll always remember her."

"Well, yes you have caught me out. Now a goodnight kiss and off to sleep and tell me about all your dreams tomorrow."